HORRiD HENRY'S
Christmas Play

HORRID HENRY'S
Christmas
Play

Francesca Simon
Illustrated by Tony Ross

Orion
Children's Books

7780 116

Horrid Henry's Christmas Play originally appeared in
Horrid Henry's Christmas Cracker first published in Great Britain in 2006
by Orion Children's Books
This edition first published in Great Britain in 2011
by Orion Children's Books
a division of the Orion Publishing Group Ltd
Orion House
5 Upper Saint Martin's Lane
London WC2H 9EA
An Hachette UK Company

1 3 5 7 9 10 8 6 4 2

Text © Francesca Simon 2006, 2011
Illustrations © Tony Ross 2011

ISBN 978 1 4440 0110 5
Printed in China.

www.orionbooks.co.uk
www.horridhenry.co.uk

*For Joshua, who knows
what it's like…*

Look out for . . .

Don't Be Horrid, Henry!
Horrid Henry's Birthday Party
Horrid Henry's Holiday
Horrid Henry's Underpants
Horrid Henry Gets Rich Quick
Horrid Henry and the Football Fiend
Horrid Henry's Nits
Horrid Henry and Moody Margaret
Horrid Henry's Thank You Letter
Horrid Henry Reads A Book
Horrid Henry's Car Journey
Moody Margaret's School
Horrid Henry Tricks and Treats

There are many more **Horrid Henry** books
available. For a complete list visit
www.horridhenry.co.uk

or

www.orionbooks.co.uk

Contents

Chapter 1

Horrid Henry slumped on the carpet and willed the clock to go faster.

Only five more minutes to hometime!
Already Henry could taste those
crisps he'd be sneaking from the
cupboard.

Miss Battle-Axe droned on about
school dinners (yuck), the new
drinking fountain,

blah blah blah,

maths homework

blah blah blah,

the school Christmas play

blah blah . . .

What? Did Miss Battle-Axe say . . .
Christmas play?
Horrid Henry sat up.

"This is a brand-new play with singing and dancing," continued Miss Battle-Axe.
"And both the older and the younger children are taking part this year."

Singing! Dancing! Showing off in front of the whole school!

Years ago, when Henry was in the infants' class, he'd played eighth sheep in the nativity play and had snatched the baby from the manger and refused to hand him back.

Henry hoped Miss Battle-Axe
wouldn't remember.
Because Henry had to play the lead.

He had to.

Who else but Henry could be
an all-singing, all-dancing Joseph?

Chapter 2

"I want to be Mary,"
shouted every girl in the class.

"I want to be a wise man!"
shouted Rude Ralph.

"I want to be a sheep!"
shouted Anxious Andrew.

"I want to be Joseph!"
shouted Horrid Henry.

"No, me!"
shouted Jazzy Jim.

"Me!"
shouted Brainy Brian.

"Quiet!" shrieked Miss Battle-Axe.
"I'm the director, and my decision
about who will act which part is final.
I've cast the play as follows:
Margaret. You will be Mary."
She handed her a thick script.

Moody Margaret whooped with joy.

All the other girls glared at her.

"Susan, front legs of the donkey;
Linda, hind legs;
cows, Fiona and Clare.
Blades of grass . . ."

Miss Battle-Axe continued
assigning parts.

Pick me for Joseph, pick me for Joseph, Horrid Henry begged silently. Who better than the best actor in the school to play the starring part?

"I'm a sheep, I'm a sheep,
I'm a beautiful sheep!"
warbled Singing Soraya.

"I'm a shepherd!"
beamed Jolly Josh.

"I'm an angel,"
trilled Magic Martha.

"I'm a blade of grass,"
sobbed Weepy William.

"Joseph will be played by . . ."

"Me!" screamed Henry.

"Me!" screamed New Nick,
Greedy Graham, Dizzy Dave
and Aerobic Al.

"Peter," said Miss Battle-Axe.
"From Miss Lovely's class."

Horrid Henry felt as if he'd been slugged in the stomach.

Perfect Peter?
His *younger* brother?

Perfect Peter
gets the starring part?

"It's not fair!" howled Horrid Henry.

Chapter 3

Miss Battle-Axe glared at him.
"Henry, you're . . ." Miss Battle-Axe
consulted her list.

Please not a blade of grass, please not
a blade of grass, prayed Horrid Henry,
shrinking. That would be just like
Miss Battle-Axe, to humiliate him.

Anything but that . . .

"... the innkeeper."
The innkeeper!

Horrid Henry sat up, beaming.
How stupid he'd been.
The innkeeper must be the
starring part. Henry could see himself
now, polishing glasses, throwing darts,
pouring out big foaming Fizzywizz
drinks to all his happy customers
while singing a song about the joys
of innkeeping.

Then he'd get into a nice long argument about why there was no room at the inn, and finally, the chance to slam the door in Moody Margaret's face after he'd pushed her away.

Wow.

Maybe he'd even get a second song.
"Ten Green Bottles" would fit right
into the story: he'd sing and dance
while knocking his less talented
classmates off a wall.
Wouldn't that be fun!

Miss Battle-Axe handed a page
to Henry.
"Your script," she said.

Henry was puzzled.
Surely there were some pages missing.
He read:

(Joseph knocks.
The innkeeper opens the door.)

JOSEPH:
Is there any room at the inn?

INNKEEPER: No

(The innkeeper shuts the door.)

Horrid Henry turned over the page.
It was blank.
He held it up to the light.
There was no secret writing.
That was it.

His entire part was one line.
One stupid puny line.
Not even a line, a word. "No."

Where was his song?

Where was his dance with the bottles
and the guests at the inn?

How could he, Horrid Henry,
the best actor in the class (and indeed,
the world) be given just one word in
the school play?

Even the donkeys got a song.

Worse, after he said his *one* word, Perfect Peter and Moody Margaret got to yack for hours about mangers and wise men and shepherds and sheep, and then sing a duet, while he, Henry, hung about behind the hay with the blades of grass.

It was so unfair!
He should be the star of the show,
not his stupid worm of a brother.

Chapter 4

Why on earth was Peter cast as Joseph anyway? He was a terrible actor. He couldn't sing, he just squeaked like a squished toad.

And why was Margaret playing Mary?
Now she'd never stop bragging
and swaggering.

AAARRRRGGGGHHHH!

"Isn't it exciting!" said Mum.

"Isn't it thrilling!" said Dad.
"Our little boy, the star of the show."

"Well done, Peter," said Mum.

"We're so proud of you," said Dad.

Perfect Peter smiled modestly.
"Of course I'm not really the star,"
he said. "Everyone's important,
even little parts like the blades of grass
and the innkeeper."

Horrid Henry pounced.
He was a Great White shark
lunging for the kill.

"AAAARRRRGGGHH!"

squealed Peter. "Henry bit me!"

"Henry! Don't be horrid!"
snapped Mum.

"Henry! Go to your room!"
snapped Dad.

Horrid Henry stomped upstairs
and slammed the door.
How could he bear the humiliation
of playing the innkeeper when
Peter was the star?

He'd just have to force Peter to
switch roles with him.
Henry was sure he could find
a way to persuade Peter, but
persuading Miss Battle-Axe was
a different matter.

Miss Battle-Axe had a mean,
horrible way of never doing what
Henry wanted.
Maybe he could trick Peter into
leaving the show.

Yes!

And then nobly offer to replace him.

Chapter 5

But unfortunately, there was
no guarantee Miss Battle-Axe
would give Henry Peter's role.
She'd probably just replace
Peter with Goody-Goody Gordon.
He was stuck.

And then Henry had a brilliant,
spectacular idea.

Why hadn't he thought of this before?
If he couldn't play a bigger part,
he'd just have to make his part bigger.
For instance, he could scream

"No."

That would get a reaction.

Or he could bellow "No,"
and then hit Joseph.
I'm an angry innkeeper, thought
Horrid Henry, and I hate guests
coming to my inn.
Certainly smelly ones like Joseph.

Or he could shout "No!",
hit Joseph, then rob him.
I'm a robber innkeeper,
thought Henry.

Or, I'm a robber
pretending to
be an innkeeper.
That would
liven up the
play a bit.

Maybe he
could be a
French robber
innkeeper, shout
"Non," and
rob Mary and
Joseph.

Or he was a French robber pirate innkeeper, so he could shout "Non," tie Mary and Joseph up and make them walk the plank.

Hmmm, thought Horrid Henry.
Maybe my part won't be so small.

After all, the innkeeper *was* the
most important character.

Rehearsals had been going
on forever.
Horrid Henry spent most
of his time slumping in a chair.
He'd never seen such a boring play.

Naturally he'd done everything
he could do to improve it.
"Can't I add a dance?" asked Henry.

"No," snapped
Miss Battle-Axe.

"Can't I add a teeny-weeny-little song?" Henry pleaded.

"No!" said Miss Battle-Axe.

"But how does the innkeeper *know* there's no room?" said Henry. "I think I should . . ."

Miss Battle-Axe glared at him with her red eyes.

"One more word from you, Henry, and you'll change places with Linda," snapped Miss Battle-Axe. "Blades of grass, let's try again . . ."

Eeek!

An innkeeper with one word was
definitely better than being invisible
as the hind legs of a donkey.

Still – it was so unfair.
He was only trying to help.

Chapter 6

Showtime!

Not a tea towel was to be found
in any local shop. Mums and dads
had been up all night frantically
sewing costumes.
Now the waiting and the
rehearsing were over. Everyone lined
up on stage behind the curtain.

Peter and Margaret waited on
the side to make their big entrance
as Mary and Joseph.

"Isn't it exciting, Henry, being in a
real play?" whispered Peter.

"No," snarled Henry.

"Places, everyone, for the opening song," hissed Miss Battle-Axe. "Now remember, don't worry if you make a little mistake. Just carry on and no one will notice."

"But I still think I should have an argument with Mary and Joseph about whether there's room," said Henry. "Shouldn't I at least check to see . . ."

"No!" snapped Miss Battle-Axe,
glaring at him.
"If I hear another peep from you
Henry, you will sit behind the bales
of hay and Jim will play your part.
Blades of grass! Line up with the
donkeys! Sheep! Get ready to baaa . . .
Bert! Are you a sheep
or a blade of grass?"

"I dunno," said Beefy Bert.

Mrs Oddbod went to the front
of the stage.
"Welcome everyone, mums and dads,
boys and girls, to our new
Christmas play, a little different from
previous years. We hope you all enjoy
a brand new show!"

Miss Battle-Axe started the CD player.

The music peeled.

The curtain rose.

The audience stamped and cheered.

Stars twinkled.

Cows mooed.

Horses neighed.

Sheep baa'ed.

Cameras flashed.

Horrid Henry stood in the wings and watched the shepherds do their Highland dance.

He still hadn't decided for sure
how he was going to play his part.
There were so many possibilities.
It was so hard to choose.

Finally, Henry's big moment arrived.
He strode across the stage and waited
behind the closed inn door for
Mary and Joseph.

Knock!
Knock! Knock! Knock!

The innkeeper stepped forward and opened the door. There was Moody Margaret, simpering away as Mary, and Perfect Peter looking full of himself as Joseph.

"Is there any room at the inn?" asked Joseph.

Good question,
thought Horrid Henry.
His mind was blank. He'd thought of
so many great things he *could* say that
what he was *supposed* to say had just
gone straight out of his head.

"Is there any room at the inn?"
repeated Joseph loudly.

"Yes," said the innkeeper.
"Come on in."

Joseph looked at Mary.
Mary looked at Joseph.

The audience murmured.

Oops, thought Horrid Henry.
Now he remembered. He'd been
supposed to say no. Oh well,
in for a penny, in for a pound.

The innkeeper grabbed Mary and
Joseph's sleeves and yanked them
through the door. "Come on in,
I haven't got all day."

"... But ... but ... the inn's full,"
said Mary.

"No it isn't," said the innkeeper.

"Is too."

"Is not. It's my inn and I should know.
This is the best inn in Bethlehem,
we've got TVs and beds, and . . ."
the innkeeper paused for a moment.
What did inns have in them?
" . . . and computers!"

Mary glared at the innkeeper.
The innkeeper glared at Mary.
Miss Battle-Axe gestured frantically
from the wings.

Chapter 7

"This inn looks full to me,"
said Mary firmly. "Come on, Joseph,
let's go to the stable."

"Oh, don't go there, you'll get fleas,"
said the innkeeper.

"So?" said Mary.

"I love fleas," said Joseph weakly.

"And it's full of manure."

"So are you," snapped Mary.

"Don't be horrid, Mary,"
said the innkeeper severely.
"Now sit down and rest your weary
bones and I'll sing you a song."
And the innkeeper started singing:

"Ten green bottles,

Standing on a wall

Ten green bottles,

Standing on a wall,

And if one green bottle Should

accidentally fall . . ."

"Ooohhh!" moaned Mary.
"I'm having the baby."

"Can't you wait till I've finished my song?" snapped the innkeeper.

"No!" bellowed Mary.

Miss Battle-Axe drew her hand across
her throat.

Henry ignored her.
After all, the show must go on.

"Come on, Joseph," interrupted Mary.
"We're going to the stable."

"OK," said Joseph.

"You're making a big mistake,"
said the innkeeper.
"We've got satellite TV and . . ."

Miss Battle-Axe ran on stage
and nabbed him.

"Thank you, innkeeper, your other
guests need you now,"
said Miss Battle-Axe, grabbing him
by the collar.

"Merry Christmas!" shrieked Horrid
Henry as she yanked him off-stage.

There was a long silence.

"Bravo!"
yelled Moody Margaret's deaf aunt.

Mum and Dad weren't sure what to
do. Should they clap, or run away to
a place where no one knew them?

Mum clapped.
Dad hid his face in his hands.

"Do you think anyone noticed?"
whispered Mum.

Dad looked at Mrs Oddbod's
grim face.

He sank down in his chair.
Maybe one day he would learn
how to make himself invisible.

"But what was I *supposed* to do?"
said Horrid Henry afterwards
in Mrs Oddbod's office.
"It's not my fault I forgot my line.
Miss Battle-Axe said not to worry
if we made a mistake and just to
carry on."

Could he help it if a star was born?

HORRID HENRY BOOKS

Horrid Henry
Horrid Henry and the Secret Club
Horrid Henry Tricks the Tooth Fairy
Horrid Henry's Nits
Horrid Henry Gets Rich Quick
Horrid Henry's Haunted House
Horrid Henry and the Mummy's Curse
Horrid Henry's Revenge
Horrid Henry and the Bogey Babysitter
Horrid Henry's Stinkbomb
Horrid Henry's Underpants
Horrid Henry Meets the Queen
Horrid Henry and the Mega-Mean Time Machine
Horrid Henry and the Football Fiend
Horrid Henry's Christmas Cracker
Horrid Henry and the Abominable Snowman
Horrid Henry Robs the Bank
Horrid Henry Wakes the Dead
Horrid Henry Rocks
Horrid Henry and the Zombie Vampire

Colour books

Horrid Henry's Big Bad Book
Horrid Henry's Wicked Ways
Horrid Henry's Evil Enemies
Horrid Henry Rules the World
Horrid Henry's House of Horrors
Horrid Henry's Dreadful Deeds
Horrid Henry Shows Who's Boss

Joke Books

Horrid Henry's Joke Book
Horrid Henry's Jolly Joke Book
Horrid Henry's Mighty Joke Book
Horrid Henry's Hilariously Horrid Joke Book
Horrid Henry's Purple Hand Gang Joke Book

Early Readers

Don't be Horrid, Henry
Horrid Henry's Birthday Party
Horrid Henry's Holiday
Horrid Henry's Underpants
Horrid Henry Gets Rich Quick
Horrid Henry and the Football Fiend
Horrid Henry's Nits
Horrid Henry and Moody Margaret
Horrid Henry's Thank You Letter
Horrid Henry Reads a Book
Horrid Henry's Car Journey
Moody Margaret's School
Horrid Henry Tricks and Treats

Horrid Henry is also available on CD and as a digital download, all read by Miranda Richardson.

HORRID HENRY
Tricks and Treats

Horrid Henry loves Hallowe'en.
He can't wait to go trick or treating.
But surely Mum doesn't expect him to
go out with Peter dressed as a
fluffy pink bunny?

MOODY MARGARET'S
School

Why should Horrid Henry spend
his precious Saturday playing
schools with Moody Margaret?
There MUST be a way he can get
sent home . . . But how?

HORRiD HENRY'S
Car Journey

Horrid Henry would much rather
be at Ralph's Goo Shooter party than
on his way to a boring christening.
So watch out, Mum and Dad,
because Henry will do ANYTHING
to stop this journey!

HORRiD HENRY
Reads a Book

A reading competition? No way.
But when Henry hears the prize is a
family ticket to a theme park.
Henry is determined to win . . .
but how on earth is he going
to read all those books?

HORRiD HENRY'S
Thank You Letter

Horrid Henry hates writing
thank you letters. Why should he
thank people for terrible presents?
Then he has a wonderful idea –
one that will make him rich, rich, rich!

HORRiD HENRY and MOODY MARGARET

Horrid Henry and Moody
Margaret are sworn enemies.
That is, until they find a common
interest – Glop! There's chaos
in the kitchen and Perfect Peter
is in for a surprise.